I Really Do Have a Dragon!

Level 10 – White

BookLife

Helpful Hints for Reading at Home

The focus phonemes (units of sound) used throughout this series are in line with the order in which your child is taught at school. This offers a consistent approach to learning whether reading at home or in the classroom.

HERE ARE SOME COMMON WORDS THAT YOUR CHILD MIGHT FIND TRICKY:

water	where	would	know	thought	through	couldn't
laughed	eyes	once	we're	school	can't	our

TOP TIPS FOR HELPING YOUR CHILD TO READ:

- Encourage your child to read aloud as well as silently to themselves.
- Allow your child time to absorb the text and make comments.
- Ask simple questions about the text to assess understanding.
- Encourage your child to clarify the meaning of new vocabulary.

This book focuses on developing independence, fluency and comprehension. It is a white level 10 book band.

I Really Do Have a Dragon!

Written by
Kirsty Holmes

Illustrated by
Silvia Nencini

Chapter One

Angelica

My name is Candice Clarke. I am eight. I have curly hair and eyes the colour of conkers. I live in a colourful caravan with Pa, Ma, and my little brother, Cody.

We move around a lot because my dad works for the Lilac Brothers' Funfair and Carnival! That's why we live in a caravan.

Pa calls me Princess. I wish I was a princess in a castle with a crown. I don't care about going to dances or kissing princes. But if I was a princess...

I would have a pet dragon!
I love dragons.
If I had a pet dragon I would climb on his back and fly away. Up, up through the clouds, climbing higher and higher, and it wouldn't be scary. It would be exciting!
"Higher, Spike!"

This is my cat. She's called Angelica.
I wish Angelica was a dragon. But dragons
don't eat cat food or catch mice and cats don't
have wings or breathe fire.

One night, Ma called me out of the caravan very late – after nine o'clock! Cody was asleep in his cot.

"What is it, Ma?" I asked.

"Come and see," she whispered quietly.

Angelica was curled up in a crate in the space underneath the caravan. It was dark, so Ma shone her lantern so that I could see.
"What's she doing?" I asked.
"Can't you see?" said Ma, holding the lantern closer.
Angelica had had kittens!

The kittens were small and their eyes were closed. Ma said we had to leave Angelica alone, so she could look after them.
Ma cooked Angelica a bit of fish and put it near the crate.
"She needs to recover," said Ma. "Having babies is no picnic!"
Clever Angelica!

A few weeks later, as I got back from the carnival, Angelica crept out from under the caravan. Right behind her was a line of perfect, tiny kittens! The kittens had adorable little faces and had lots of fur.

But hang on a second... The last kitten was... different.

It wasn't fluffy. And it didn't have a cute button nose, or whiskers.

It did have a long, spiky tail, though.

And it had tiny wings.

A wisp of smoke curled from its nose.

I couldn't believe it.

This was EPIC!

The last kitten wasn't a kitten at all. It was a dragon!

I scooped him up in my arms and ran into the caravan.

"Ma! Pa! Look!"

"Cat!" said Cody.

"No, Cody," said Ma. "Can you say 'dragon'?"

"Cat!" said Cody, again.

I couldn't believe there was an actual dragon in my caravan!

"Can I keep him?" I asked. I pulled a cute face so they would say yes.

"If you take care of him, Princess, then yes," said Pa.

"He'll be excellent at catching mice!" said Ma.

"Cat!" said Cody, pressing his face close to my dragon.

I knew it! I was a secret princess all along! The dragon was clear evidence.

"What are you going to call him?" asked Pa.

"I have already decided," I said. "His name is Spike."

Chapter Two

I Really Do Have a Dragon!

I really did have a dragon at last!
I couldn't wait to get to school the next day.
Whenever the carnival moves on, I go to a new
school. Making friends isn't easy. I couldn't
wait to see everyone's faces when I told them
about Spike!

I told my class that I had a pet dragon, and that his name was Spike. I waited for them to be amazed...

But they didn't believe me!

"Oh, be realistic," said Emily. "Dragons don't exist, Candice."

"But I really do have a dragon!" I said.

Spike got bigger and bigger. He clung to my shoulder, blowing cute little puffs of smoke. I begged Pa to let me take him to school. "Dragons don't belong in class, Princess," he said.

"Candice? What made these holes in your cardigan?" my teacher, Mr Martin, asked.
"Spike's claws," I said.
"And who is Spike?" asked Mr Martin, curiously.
"He's my dragon. His claws are sharp," I said.
"Oh," said Mr Martin. "A dragon! What a magical and unrealistic pet!"
Clearly he didn't believe me either.

Back at home, I asked Ma if I could take Spike to school.

"Of course not," said Ma. "He's a decent size now. Imagine the havoc he'd cause in a classroom!"

"Please?" I made the cute face again.

"Listen to your Ma, Princess. It's not a good idea," said Pa.

"Maybe Spike can help you with your homework?" said Pa, nicely.
Spike tried to help with my English work. I wrote a story about a princess in a castle and her dragon, Spike. They flew through the clouds together, swooping through the air.

Spike blew little circles of smoke. I gave him a cookie.

"Cat!" said Cody.

"Can you say Spike?" I said.

"Cat!" said Cody, reaching for Spike's tail.

"Candice? What happened to your homework?" called Mr Martin in class the next day.

"It caught fire, Mr Martin," I said.

"Was it Spike, again?" asked Mr Martin.

"Of course, Mr Martin," I said. "Cody pulled his tail, and then he coughed."

"And scorched your homework?" said Mr Martin. "Oh, Candice."

I was angry all through our music class. Why wouldn't anyone believe me?

Ma said it might have been because some people don't believe that dragons are real.

"Most people think magic is only real in books," said Ma.

"Poor them!" said Pa. "Imagine being so completely boring!"

At home, Spike became my best friend. The best thing about Spike was that I wouldn't have to leave him behind when the Lilac Brothers moved the carnival to the next place. He could come with us and live in the caravan.

One day, Spike and I could have an act in the carnival!

I could just picture it.

Princess Candice and her dragon, Spike! Come and see how they fly and swoop! Applaud as they dive through the air!

Chapter Three

Pets Day

One day, Mr Martin sent a very, very exciting letter home from school.

It said:

Dear Parents
This Friday, our class will have Pets Day.
Children can bring small pets, such as hamsters, in cages into class.
No cats, dogs or chickens please.
From
Mr Martin

"I can finally take Spike to school!" I cried.
"Only if you can cram him in a cage, Princess!"
said Pa.
I looked at Spike. He was much bigger than a
cat, or a dog.
"You could take your stick insects?" said Ma.
"Sure," I said. "Sorry, Spike."

"Bye, Ma! Bye, Pa!" I called as I ran out of the door.

"Hang on!" called Pa. "You forgot your stick insects!"

"Thanks, Pa," I said.

"Princess?" said Pa. "You've got a lot to carry today."

"That's... um... my swimming costume," I said. "There's an extra class today."

I carried on running as if nothing had happened. My heart was racing, and I could feel my cheeks turning red.
I'm not very good at keeping secrets, especially from Pa.

I crept into school and hung Spike on the back of my chair. I put the stick insects on my desk. "Which one is Spike?" asked Mr Martin, putting his face close to the cage. "Is he here?"

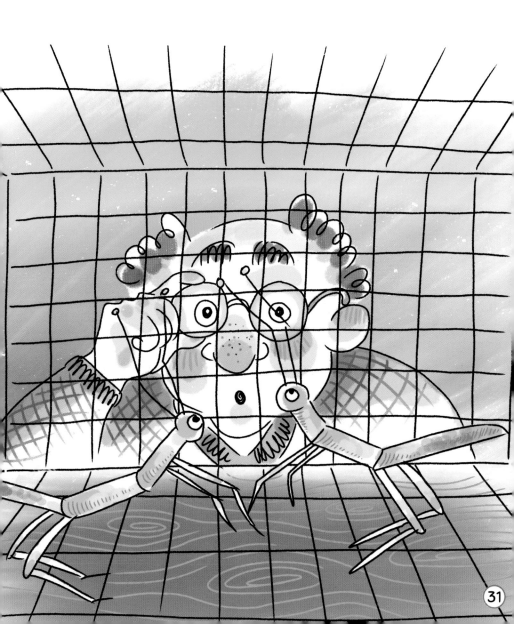

"Um... sort of," I said, crossing my fingers.
One by one, we were called to the front of the class to show off our pets.
Most of the pets were cute, but boring.
"My rabbit is called Elsa," said Lucy. "She likes to eat carrots."

$$12 + 11 = 23$$
$$120 + 110 = 230$$
$$10 + 30 = 40$$

"This is Ralph," said James. "He is a mouse. He likes to climb."
Ralph climbed up into James' hair.
I could hear Spike moving behind me. It was almost our turn. I put the stick insects under my desk.

"A mouse is great," I thought. "But can he breathe fire?"

"Candice, would you like to come up next?" said Mr Martin. "You've brought something very cool to show us all, haven't you?"

"I certainly have, Mr Martin," I said.

I walked to the front of the class.

I whistled.

"Spike? Come!" I called.

Spike flew out of the bag and swooped across
the classroom, just like we'd practised.
Spike was AMAZING!
He flew round the room and then landed,
clinging to my arm.
I looked around at a room of amazed faces.
"This is Spike," I said. "See? I really do have a
dragon!"

When I got home that afternoon, Ma and Pa were waiting for me.
I smiled at them.
"Ma! Can I have my new friends over to play? Can I go to Emily's house? James wants to come for tea. Is that OK?" I cried.

Pa smiled.

"OK, Princess Popular. Of course you can," he said.

"Did Spike have a nice day at school?" asked Ma, smiling.

"Spike is the best," I said proudly. "He had the best time. And so did I."

"Spike!" cried Cody, at last.

I really, really do have a dragon, you know.

I Really Do Have a Dragon!

1.   How old is Candice?

2.   What happened to Candice's homework?
       (a) Spike ate it
       (b) It caught fire
       (c) She left it at home

3.   Why didn't Candice tell Ma and Pa she was taking Spike
       into school for Pets Day?

4.   What animal had James brought in to school for Pets
       Day?

5.   Why do you think nobody believed Candice that she
       really had a dragon? Would you have believed her?

©2020 **BookLife Publishing Ltd.**
King's Lynn, Norfolk PE30 4LS

ISBN 978–1–83927–018–5

All rights reserved. Printed in Malaysia.
A catalogue record for this book is available
from the British Library.

I Really Do Have a Dragon!
Written by Kirsty Holmes
Illustrated by Silvia Nencini

An Introduction to BookLife Readers...

Our Readers have been specifically created in line with the London Institute of Education's approach to book banding and are phonetically decodable and ordered to support each phase of the Letters and Sounds document.

Each book has been created to provide the best possible reading and learning experience. Our aim is to share our love of books with children, providing both emerging readers and prolific page-turners with beautiful books that are guaranteed to provoke interest and learning, regardless of ability.

BOOK BAND GRADED using the Institute of Education's approach to levelling.

PHONETICALLY DECODABLE supporting each phase of Letters and Sounds.

EXERCISES AND QUESTIONS to offer reinforcement and to ascertain comprehension.

BEAUTIFULLY ILLUSTRATED to inspire and provoke engagement, providing a variety of styles for the reader to enjoy whilst reading through the series.

AUTHOR INSIGHT:
KIRSTY HOLMES

Kirsty Holmes, holder of a BA, PGCE, and an MA, was born in Norfolk, England. She has written over 60 books for BookLife Publishing, and her stories are full of imagination, creativity and fun.

This book focuses on developing independence, fluency and comprehension. It is a white level 10 book band.